*Dayenu* is a reminder to be aware of and grateful for the blessings in each moment.

To my son Jeff, for finding the bitter herbs. Also to
Marietta B. Zacker, Sonya Sones, Ruth Lercher Bornstein,
Lyra Halprin and the Thirds; and especially to Kathe
Pinchuck, Barbara Bietz and Susan Dubin: toda raba!
—A.H.W.

To my husband and family.
Many thanks to Temple Beth Shalom in Hickory, N.C.,
for welcoming me with open arms and teaching me
how to eat gefilte fish.
—K.K.

Dial Books for Young Readers
Penguin Young Readers Group
An Imprint of Penguin Random House LLC
375 Hudson Street
New York, NY 10014

Text Copyright © 2016 by April Halprin Wayland • Illustrations © 2016 by Katie Kath

Library of Congress Cataloging-in-Publication Data

Wayland, April Halprin.
More than enough / by April Halprin Wayland ; illustrated by Katie Kath.    pages cm
Summary: Illustrations and simple text portray children and their family as they prepare for, then celebrate, a Passover
seder with foods, games, songs, and even a sleepover.
ISBN 978-0-8037-4126-3 (hardcover)
[1. Passover—Fiction. 2. Seder—Fiction. 3. Judaism—Customs and practices—Fiction. 4. Family life—Fiction.]
I. Kath, Katie, illustrator. II. Title.
PZ7.W35126Mor 2016    [E]—dc23    2014049277

Manufactured in China on acid-free paper
3 5 7 9 10 8 6 4 2

Designed by Mina Chung • Text set in Chaloops
This art was created using watercolor paint.

Special Markets ISBN 978-0-3991-8632-5 • CIP 032130.7K2/B0795/A3

# More Than Enough

## A Passover Story

by April Halprin Wayland

illustrated by Katie Kath

Dial Books for Young Readers

We wander the market
surrounded by colors—

*Dayenu*

We buy apples and walnuts,
lilacs and honey—
*dayenu*

We reach through the bars
to lift one purring kitten.

He licks Mama's nose

so she says we can
keep him—

dayenu

Wait . . . is that rain?
Yes, it's *rain*, we can taste it!

# dayenu

Kitten meets Daddy
as we carry in groceries—

dayenu

We chop apples and walnuts
and mix in the grape juice—
*dayenu*

We soak in blue bubbles

and dress up for dinner—

*dayenu*

We dash through the puddles
with our bowl of charoset—

dayenu

We skip into Nana's
and show who we've rescued—

*dayenu*

We set out the plate
filled with symbols of freedom—
dayenu

We ask the four questions
and all sing Dayenu—

dayenu

There are matzoh balls, chicken,
and jellied fruit slices—

*dayenu*

We search high and low

for the lost afikomen—

dayenu

We open the door for Elijah,
the prophet.

And baa like a goat
singing *Chad Gadya*'s verses—

*dayenu*

We play with our kitten
'til Nana says bedtime.

She wraps us in blankets,
then sings *Eliyahu*—

*dayenu*

Her kiss on our foreheads,

a purring warm kitten,

a feast in our tummies,

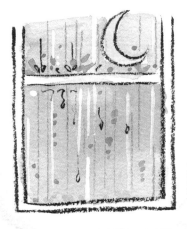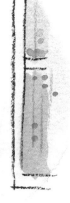

night rain at the window,

a Passover sleepover.

Dayenu...
    dayenu...
        dayenu!

**Dayenu:** A joyous Passover song. Dayenu means "it would have been enough." It is a thanksgiving song for all that was given to the Jewish people, proclaiming that any one of the gifts (such as leading them out of slavery, parting the Red Sea, and the giving of the Torah) would have been enough. It is a reminder to be aware of and grateful for the blessings in each moment.

**Afikomen:** A piece of matzoh that is hidden during the seder and without which the seder cannot end; the one who finds it may receive a small reward.

***Chad Gadya***: A playful and symbolic song about a little goat that's sung at the end of the seder, often with sound effects.

**Charoset:** A mixture, often made of apples or dates, nuts, cinnamon, honey, and wine or grape juice, symbolizing the mortar Jewish slaves used when they built structures for the Egyptians.

**Elijah**: A prophet for whom a door is opened during the seder, inviting him to enter. This signifies the hope for Elijah's return to earth, said to usher in an age of peace. The song *Eliyahu Hanavi—Elijah the Prophet*—is a Passover favorite.

**Haggadah** ("the telling" in Hebrew): A small book used at the Passover seder that includes the order of the ritual meal, the story of the Israelites' escape from slavery in Egypt, poetry, and songs.

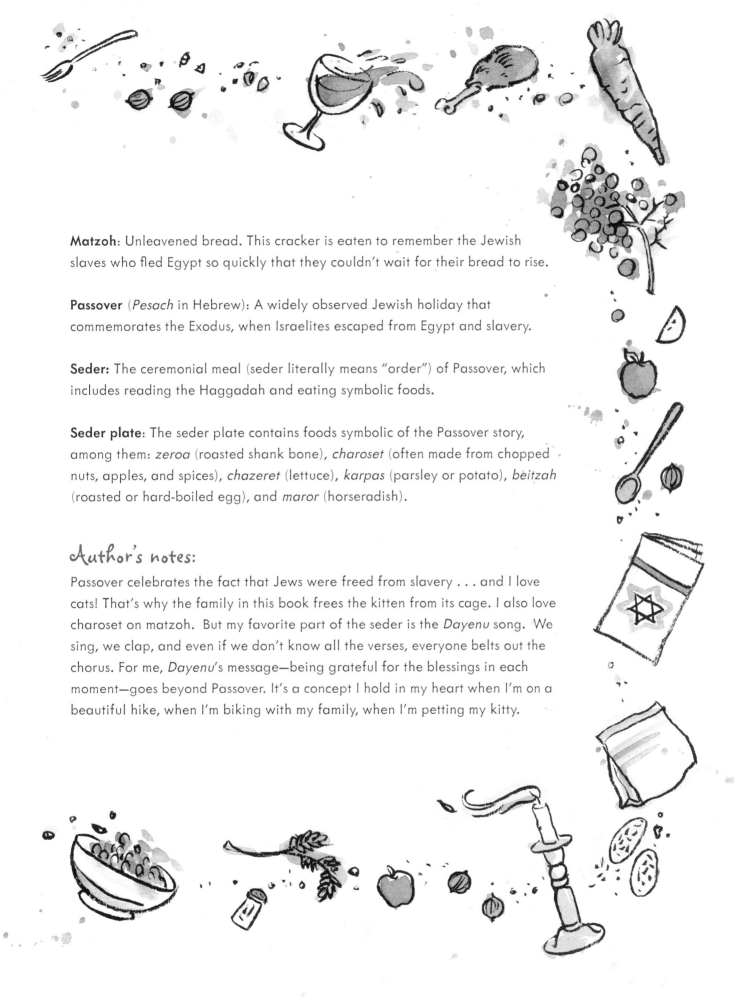

**Matzoh**: Unleavened bread. This cracker is eaten to remember the Jewish slaves who fled Egypt so quickly that they couldn't wait for their bread to rise.

**Passover** (*Pesach* in Hebrew): A widely observed Jewish holiday that commemorates the Exodus, when Israelites escaped from Egypt and slavery.

**Seder**: The ceremonial meal (seder literally means "order") of Passover, which includes reading the Haggadah and eating symbolic foods.

**Seder plate**: The seder plate contains foods symbolic of the Passover story, among them: *zeroa* (roasted shank bone), *charoset* (often made from chopped nuts, apples, and spices), *chazeret* (lettuce), *karpas* (parsley or potato), *beitzah* (roasted or hard-boiled egg), and *maror* (horseradish).

### Author's notes:

Passover celebrates the fact that Jews were freed from slavery . . . and I love cats! That's why the family in this book frees the kitten from its cage. I also love charoset on matzoh.  But my favorite part of the seder is the *Dayenu* song.  We sing, we clap, and even if we don't know all the verses, everyone belts out the chorus. For me, *Dayenu*'s message—being grateful for the blessings in each moment—goes beyond Passover. It's a concept I hold in my heart when I'm on a beautiful hike, when I'm biking with my family, when I'm petting my kitty.

# Dayenu

I - lu ho-tzi   ho-tzi-a - nu,      ho-tzi-a - nu      mi-mitz-ra - yim,

ho - tzi-a - nu      mi - mitz-ra - yim      da - yei - nu.

(Chorus) Da - da - yei-nu,_____ da - da - yei-nu,_____ da-da -yei-nu,   da-

yei-nu da-yei- nu da-yei-nu.      yei-nu da-yei - nu.

# The Story of Passover

The first Passover happened long ago in the far-away country of Egypt. A mean and powerful king, called Pharaoh, ruled Egypt. Worried that the Jewish people would one day fight against him, Pharaoh decided that these people must become his slaves. As slaves, the Jewish people worked very hard. Every day, from morning until night, they hammered, dug, and carried heavy bricks. They built palaces and cities and worked without rest. The Jewish people hated being slaves. They cried and asked God for help. God chose a man named Moses to lead the Jewish people. Moses went to Pharaoh and said, "God is not happy with the way you treat the Jewish people. He wants you to let the Jewish people leave Egypt and go into the desert, where they will be free." But Pharaoh stamped his foot and shouted, "No, I will never let the Jewish people go!" Moses warned, "If you do not listen to God, many terrible things, called plagues, will come to your land." But Pharaoh would not listen, and so the plagues arrived. First, the water turned to blood. Next, frogs and, later, wild animals ran in and out of homes. Balls of hail fell from the sky and bugs, called locusts, ate all of the Egyptians' food.

Each time a new plague began, Pharaoh would cry, "Moses, I'll let the Jewish people go. Just stop this horrible plague!" Yet no sooner would God take away the plague than Pharaoh would shout: "No, I've changed my mind. The Jews must stay!" So God sent more plagues. Finally, as the tenth plague arrived, Pharaoh ordered the Jews to leave Egypt.

Fearful that Pharaoh might again change his mind, the Jewish people packed quickly. They had no time to prepare food and no time to allow their dough to rise into puffy bread. They had only enough time to make a flat, cracker-like bread called matzah. They hastily tied the matzah to their backs and ran from their homes.

The people had not travelled far before Pharaoh commanded his army to chase after them and bring them back to Egypt. The Jews dashed forward, but stopped when they reached a large sea. The sea was too big to swim across. Frightened that Pharaoh's men would soon reach them, the people prayed to God, and a miracle occurred. The sea opened up. Two walls of water stood in front of them and a dry, sandy path stretched between the walls. The Jews ran across. Just as they reached the other side, the walls of water fell and the path disappeared. The sea now separated the Jews from the land of Egypt. They were free!

Each year at Passover, we eat special foods, sing songs, tell stories, and participate in a seder — a special meal designed to help us remember this miraculous journey from slavery to freedom.